BL

by

Robbie Moffat

PALM TREE PUBLISHING

PALM TREE PUBLISHING
Iver Grove, Iver SL0 0LB

© Robbie Moffat 2021

First published in paperback
FEBRUARY 2021

Typeset: Verdana 12pt

ISBN-10: 0 907282 80 6
ISBN-13: 9780907282808

PREFACE

This story is about faith, ignorance, denial and revenge. In parts it is about unity, common purpose, and triumphalism. However, it is also about sadistic nature, power gone wrong, and retribution.

For this kind of story is for an audience obsessed with religious wrong-doing, its hypocrisy and its secrets. If there is a moral, then it must be that the reader following the actions of our heroine understand why she is compelled to commit the same acts that have been perpetrated on her.

Only after such deeds are done, when the meaning of compassion is fully understood, can our heroine change the course of her life and of those that she leads.

DEDICATION

For all those who are good.

1

A lonely part of Flanders, 1928. Rooks are settled in the trees. A gunshot goes off. The birds rise into the sky - circle the fields below.

A long deserted tree-lined road. In the distance - a village with a church spire dominating the skyline. Nina Hager, a young mother is pushing a pram containing a crying two year old baby. She is dragging her difficult four year old girl Liesbeth by the hand as she struggles up the long road towards the looming abbey.

The abbey is shuttered and foreboding. Nina pounds with her fist on the large iron gate that stands broodingly in the break of the high brick wall that surrounds the entire complex of buildings. She impatiently rocks the pram to and fro to quieten the baby as Liesbeth plays in the dirt.
There is silence. Nina, angry and impatient, pounds on the iron gate again.

*

Inside the abbey in the expansive courtyard fringed by the high walls, five tunic attired Cistercian nuns are playing with a football. The ball is mis-kicked and lands at the calipered foot of Sister Maria Marlier. Aged thirty two, her skin is smooth and unwrinked, her eyes serene and smiling.

Sister Lutgard Smeets, also thirty two, mischievous by nature and temperament, shouts to her.

"To me, Maria! To me!"

Sisters Petra Belet, Juliana Rutten, and Harlindis Gerits try to block her as Maria kicks the ball to Lutgard. They fail and Lutgard dribbles the ball past Harlindis.

"Lutgard! Back to me!" Maria bellows. She moves swiftly in spite of her crippled leg.

*

Nina is still pounding on the door. Both children are crying. There is a sound of a key turning in a lock. The door swings open. Sister Heleen Steylaers the porter, in her mid-thirties, looks out.

"Yes ... Can I help you?"

Nina is contemptuous "Where is the bitch!" She grabs Liesbeth by the arm and pushes the pram past the Sister. Heleen is placid but agitated by the intrusion. She closes the gate.

*

A small ill-lid anti-room. Sister Idesbalda Van Soest is nursing Nina's baby in her arms. Sister Humbelina Roelandts is reading to little Liesbeth who has a short attention span and is fidgeting.

"And then Jesus put his hands on the sick man ... Are you listening, Liesbeth?"

Idesbalda is more experienced with children. "The poor child is hungry, Humbelina. You hold the baby and I'll fetch some cakes from the kitchen."

Humbelina takes hold of the baby awkwardly. "What if she starts crying?"

"Talk to her ..... she is a little sack stuffed with divinity."

Idesbalda leaves for the kitchen.

Abbess Agnes Swevers, fifties, Prioress Lucia Delaere, forties, and sister Heleen, stand before Nina who is in a rage.

"One of you is having sex with my man! I'll swear it on a bible. Give me a bible!" Nina searches the room frantically. "You don't even have a bible!" She flops on the floor in despair. Lucia and Heleen stoop to pick her up.

"What you are saying is not possible ..." Abbess Agnes stares coldly.

Nina stares at the Abbess with a loathing. "What do you mean??? You're women, arn't you?"

"Not your kind of woman" Lucia retorts with a snarl.

Agnes holds up her hand to silence Lucia. "We are sisters. The brides of Christ. Being desired, or pursuing a man is alien to us in our devotion to God's only son."

Nina is mocking. "Don't give me that! One of you has been servicing the father of my children!"

Lucia is incensed by the accusation. "You are making no sense, you stupid woman!"

Agnes is shocked by Lucia's outburst. "Forgive the Prioress's anger. Your accusation goes against all that we hold dear, my child."

Heleen reaches for Nina's hand. "You must be mistaken."

Nina shakes off Heleen's attempted approach. "I'm mistaken for coming here! I knew I wouldn't get the truth from a bunch of spinsters!"

Lucia and Heleen look to Agnes. She meets their gaze but does not react. She is weak. Her eyes slowly return to settle on Nina. "In good faith, we will enquire into the matter."

"Then what? Are you going to ex-communicate her???"

Lucia loses her reserve. "That is enough! Sister Heleen with show you out."

Nina turns to Agnes. "Are you in charge here or what????"

Agnes is visibly unable to summon the strength to assert her authority. "We will look into it ...

"You lot are all the same. You stick together like sheep in a pen!"

Heleen takes Nina by the arm to guide her to the door. Nina shrugs her off and snatches the large bunch of keys dangling from Heleen's belt. "Touch me again and I'll knock your teeth out with these!"

Heleen remains docile. "We are forbidden to defend ourselves. Do

what you must. God is our judge."
"You're a bunch of cows!"
Nina thrusts Heleen's keys back at her - pushes her way out.

*

The rooks are back in the trees. The door of the abbey BANGS shut. The sound of the key turning.

Nina stands on the empty road. She is defiant. "You hypocrites! God damn you all!" Nina spits on the ground in contempt. With Liesbeth in one hand, she starts to push the pram with her other hand back towards the village. Liesbeth looks innocently back to the abbey as she nibbles on a cake.

2

Its is evening. Thirty nuns are gathered in the great hall. There is a small buzz of excited whispering. Maria and Lutgard with sisters Petra, Juliana, and Harlindis, are huddled together on the backless benches set out in rows in front of a low dais supporting the Abbess's carved oak chair.

Lutgard is matter of fact. "It'll be a purge on smoking again."

Juliana is not convinced. "Must be something bigger than that to have called a council meeting midweek."

"I hope its about the cooking" Petra moans. "Its really gone downhill the last three months since Sister Ann died."

Harlindis turns to Maria. "What do you think, Maria?" Just as Maria is about to answer, Agnes, Lucia and Heleen file into the hall. The nuns rise. Agnes and Lucia mount the low dais, Heleen stands with the other nuns. Lucia addresses the gathering. "Thank you, sisters. Please be seated."

The nuns seat themselves on the benches. Agnes settles into the carved chair. Lucia remains standing, addresses the nuns.

"Sisters. We are a community living under this roof to practice chastity, temperance, charity, diligence, patience, kindness and humility."

The nuns utter in unison "Amen!"

"Temptation is everywhere ... lust, gluttony, greed, sloth, wrath, envy and pride."

The nuns ritually reply "Amen."

Lucia gets into full flow "The renunciation of one's own will ... the arming of oneself with the strong and noble weapons of obedience under the banner of the true king, Christ Our Lord ..."

The nuns repeat in unison "Christ Our Lord" and cross themselves.

"We are a school for the Lord's service. This is our way to salvation ... through patience we share in the passion of Christ and his Kingdom."

The nuns repeat in loud voice "Christ and his Kingdom."

Lucia has played her part. She steps back, stands behind the carved chair.

Agnes holds up her hand. "Thank you, Prioress. You may be seated."

Lucia is irritated at being asked to sit with the other nuns. She excuses herself, remains standing. Agnes is perplexed by Lucia's disobedience, but lets it go as she does not want to lose face. She gets up, speaks slowly and with great deliberation.

"You know me to be a plain speaker, so I will get to the point. A grave accusation was made against our house today. Very grave. It attacks the first principle of our community - chastity. I believe it is a false accusation, but I must take private audience from each of you after supper. I will try not to keep you too late into the night. Praise be to Christ our Lord. Amen."

The nuns all stand, repeat "Christ our Lord. Amen."

*

The same small anti-room outside the Abbess's office where Nina's children had been kept. There are candles burning in long candle holders. The last group of nuns, Maria, Lutgard, Petra, Juliana, Harlindis and novice Rosa Van Den Bosch, nineteen, are waiting to be interviewed by the Abbess. They are reading their books of prayer.

"She's been in a long time" Lutgard declares.

"Be quiet, Lutgard" Maria is exasperated. "Its a serious matter."

Humbelina exits from the Abbess's room. She is smiling. Lutgard closes her prayer book. "So its not you, Sister Humbelina?"

"Certainly not, Lutgard! I hope you have your answers ready! You're next."

Lutgard half smiles, goes into the Abbess's office.

"I bet its her" Harlindis announces. "She has prior history."

Maria closes her prayer book. "I think its all a bit of a farce."

Humbelina shakes her head. "The woman was adamant. There was no disguising her anger. She said it was her man … but she wasn't wearing a wedding ring?"

Juliana is thoughtful. "Perhaps she had to sell it. Times are hard."

"Or she is lying" Petra announces boldly. "What's the name of the man?"

Humbelina feels accused. "I don't know! You are always making me out to be a fool, Petra."

Petra smiles. Juliana embraces her.
"We love you, sister Humbelina."
"Thank you, Juliana."
Juliana reproaches Petra. "You need to work on your kindness, Petra. You are not setting a good example for young Rosa."
Rosa smiles sweetly.
Petra smirks. "Young Rosa is doing just fine, arn't you?
"Yes, Sister Petra."
Harlindis is hanging on to the matter at hand. "That woman came here all the way from the village and didn't even name him? Don't you think that strange?"
Maria offers an explanation "Perhaps she's scared of him."
"Yes, Maria, but why come and say something to the Abbess in the first place if she was frightened." Harlindis asks.
"That woman was frightened of no-one!" Humbelina declares.
Maria weighs up the answers. "Women are more complex than men. God works in mysterious ways. So do women."
"That's blasphemous!"
"Sister Petra. Under all that cloth, you are a woman, and there is no

doubting that you are a constant mystery to us!"

The other nuns giggle. Petra sulks.

Lutgard comes out of the room. Petra is quick to throw a jibe at her. "That was a quick confession."

"I had nothing to confess, sister. I am not a fornicator."

Juliana is visibily mortified. "Please, Lutgard, curb your language!"

Lutgard ignores her. "You're next, Maria."

"What questions did they ask you?"

"You'll find out."

Maria goes into the room.

*

In the Abbess's room, Agnes, Lucia and Heleen are seated. Maria stands before them.

Agnes is studying Maria intently. "You work on the farm every day, daughter?"

"Most of us do, mother."

"Do you know the villager Karl Riikers?"

"Yes, I do. He helps us sell our produce."

Lucia picks up the line of questioning. "How well do you know him?"

Maria ponders her answer. "Karl? We talk about things, his family, God, you know ...."

"You are never alone with him?"

A small wrinkle appears on Maria's brow. "I've never thought about it. Yes, sometimes when we are negotiating the price of our vegetables, or in the filed discussing how to increase the yield."

Agnes picks up the questioning again. "You also know Lee Van Der Berg from the village?"

"Yes, Mother, Lee repairs our machinery."

"You are on first name terms with him too?"

"He asked me to call him Lee instead of Mr. Van Der Berg."

Lucia intercedes. "Do you speak to him about his family?"

Maria frowns. "I don't know if he has a family. We mainly talk about tractors and how to plough straight furrows."

Agnes gives a little smile. Lucia shuffles a piece of paper. "Christien Gutten? You also speak directly with him?"

Maria chooses her words carefully. "As you know, Prioress, he supplies us with our flour for the bakery."

"He comes to the abbey regularly, correct? Twice a week, sometimes more."

"Yes, Prioress. He also brings us seed and fertilizer from Antwerp."

"Are you ever alone with him?"

"Very rarely."

"So there are times you are alone with him?"

"Yes. When I pay his bill."

Lucia makes a note of this. "Do you talk intimately with him?"

Maria gives a little laugh. "If you consider the price of everything, politics and the weather as intimate, yes. He is quite interested in having my opinion on the world."

"And on our Lord Jesus? You speak to him of your devotion to our Lord?"

"Our Lord Jesus, of course. He is very religious. As you know he was once a priest."

Agnes holds up her hand to stop Lucia from asking any more questions.

"Thank you, sister Maria. You may go. Can you ask Sister Petra to come in next, please."

"Yes, Mother. Thank you."

*

Maria comes out of the room. Humbelina and Lutgard have gone. Maria gives a little bow to Petra.

"I will pray for you, Petra."

"What is that supposed to mean?"

The others are humoured by Petra's discomfort. As Petra goes into the room, she gives them all a glaring look. Harlindis hands Maria her prayer book.

"Well? How did it go?"

"They are taking the accusation very seriously."

"Do they know the man's name yet?" Rosa asks timidly.

Maria places her hand on Rosa's forehead as a blessing. "Patience, Rosa. Patience. Excuse me, sisters. I have to be in the fields extra early in the morning. Good night."

Maria departs.

Juliana settles to wait. "I don't need a man. I've met the person for me."

"Jesus our Lord ...?" Rosa asks.

Harlindis tuts. "Of course, you novice. He's known us all of our lives. Since we were little girls."

"It is his call we have heeded." Juliana lectures. "Through patience

you will know the passion of Christ.
"I can't wait!" Rosa is elated.
Juliana and Harlindis share a look of
'she'll learn'.

3

Maria, in dungarees, is driving a tractor. Lutgard similarly dressed and in wellie boots is in the field coming towards her. She waves Maria to stop. Maria switches the engine off.

"Christian Guttens is here. Do you mind if I help him unload the van at the bakery?"

Christien Guttens, a lean tall thirty something man, sits in a white lorry looking towards them.

"Are you in love with him, Lutgard?"

"Yes, aren't we all? But I'm not going to do anything about it, am I?"

"Lust is a terrible thing. Are you harbouring lustful thoughts for him?"

"A little bit. What woman doesn't struggle with that. Its not a sin to dream? He's a fine looking man."

"I would say he's trouble ..."

"I like a bit of trouble."

Heleen approaches.

"Come on, Maria, get the tractor going. We want to finish before its dark."

Maria starts the tractor. Lutgard makes towards Christien's lorry. Heleen follows her with her eyes. Pulls out a small pocketbook and makes a note.

*

The abbey shower room. The nuns are communally showering after working in the fields. Maria is under the shower-head scrubbing her short hair. Lutgard squeezes under the shower next to her.
"Want me to do that for you?"
"No, I'm fine."
Lutgard starts to sing.
"What are you so happy about?"
"Oh, I don't know. Its not sinful to be happy. Go on, soap my back."
Maria rubs Lutgard's shoulders with the soap. Lutgard's back is scarred. Maria runs her fingers along one of the scars.
"Oh that's lovely ...."
"Behave yourself."
"Its my nature to be ...."
"Frisky?"
"Sensuous. Oh isn't life wonderful! Thank you God!"
"Lutgard ....?" Heleen frowns at her. The other nuns giggle.

"Sorry …" Lutgard pulls Maria into her, whispers. "I'm so glad I came back. I missed you most of all when I went away. How's your leg?"

"It comes and goes."

"I'll massage it for you before we go to bed."

Heleen gets under the shower next to them. They push apart. Lutgard continues to sing while Maria carries on washing her hair.

*

There is an open backed lorry parked by the field. Maria, Juliana and Rosa are helping Karl Riikers, forty something, to load up with vegetable boxes. Lucia stands by earnestly watching them. Karl takes a step back and admires Lucia.

"You're looking gorgeous today, Sister Lucia."

She gives him a stony stare.

"Its the way the light catches you. You must have been quite a beauty when you were younger."

"You are a flatterer, Mr Riikers. It won't work on me."

"Nonsense, it works on every woman!"

Lucia half smiles. "The devil take

you. I won't be having you talk down the price."

Karl laughs. Maria and Juliana are placing two bicycles on the lorry with the vegetables. Karl helps them. "Hop on, sisters." Maria, Juliana and Rosa get into the back of the lorry. Lucia is puzzled.

"You only have two bicycles!"

"Rosa will share with me, Sister."

Maria waves as the lorry drives off. Heleen joins Lucia watching the lorry bump down the farm road.

"Should we not be forbidding this?"

Lucia shrugs her shoulders. "The Mother Superior doesn't believe that anything is going on."

"And you, Sister?

Lucia continues to watch the lorry as it joins the road. "I have prayed to God to show me a sign."

"The signs are there, Lucia. The sisters are too familiar with each other and the likes of Mr. Riikers. We need more punishments."

"I agree, Heleen. We have wandered off the moderate path between individual zeal and community restraint. I'm all for fostering understanding of human nature, but we must establish due order."

Heleen nods. "Indeed. But we don't have enough geographical isolation from that village."

They turn back towards the abbey.

"You think we should build a wall around the fields?"

"Our work here is being retarded by our proximity to the village."

Two sisters Roberta Koeken and Alberica Hauchecome are on top of a haystack playfully throwing hay at one another.

Lucia is appalled. "Sister Roberta!"

The two nuns stop their fun instantly. Alberica hides behind the stack.

Roberta stands stiffly. "Prioress ...."

Heleen moves around the stack. Alberica sees she has been found.

"Forgive me, Sister Heleen."

"Get down!"

Alberica does as she is told, joins Roberta in front of Lucia.

"Report to me after supper!" The two nuns appear to be terrified of what she means. "You are confined to the dormitory!"

The two sisters, bow, run off towards the abbey.

Lucia shakes her head. "You are right, Heleen. Obedience is being eroded at every turn."

"May I speak freely, sister?"

Lucia half cocks her head. "Go on?"

"Perhaps it is time for a new abbess?"

Lucia is slightly startled. Heleen casts her eyes downwards.

"You've given this some thought?"

"As Porter it is my duty to keep the abbey self contained."

"Isolated, yes."

"Autonomous. We are in a spiritual crisis. Our chastity has been questioned by an outsider. We are doing nothing about it."

Lucia listens without reacting.

"You as Prioress, I as Porter, can request an election for a new Abbess."

A flicker of possibility registers in Lucia as she avoids Heleen's eyes.

"It will be for the good of the community, Lucia."

Lucia says nothing, starts walking towards the abbey. Heleen pulls some straw off her habit, returns to the field.

4

The Riikers lorry is parked outside a small grocer store in the village. Maria, Juliana and Rosa are unloading the boxes of vegetables. Lee Van der Berg, a man in his thirties, walks up to the nuns. He is very familiar.

"You planting those furrows straight, Miss Maria?"

"I am not, Mister Van De Berg."

"She telling the truth, Miss Juliana?"

Juliana is in a fluster at being addressed by Lee. Maria is self-assured. "You know yourself, Lee, that the tracking on the front wheels have never been the same since Humbelina put it in the ditch."

"That's right, Miss Maria. When can I come and fix it for you?"

"When we've saved enough to pay you."

"You know you don't have to pay me, Maria. I'm glad to help you poor souls out there in that drafty old convent." He turns to Rosa.

"How's you getting on being a novice, Miss Rosa?"

"Alright ...."

"You not missing the bright lights

and all?"

"A bit, I suppose ..."

Juliana comes to her defense. "She'll get over it. Her generation is thirsting for a dose of orthodoxy." Rosa scowls.

"My daughters could do with a bit of discipline with their knee high dresses and high heels and their cigarettes. Ruining their beauty they are."

Rosa offers her opinion on girls her age. "Telephones and gramophones is all envy and wrath. While it is nice to stay in touch with friends, whatever new dance your daughters learn, it won't fulfill them. All they'll want is more." Maria and Juliana are amused by Rosa's outburst. "Renouncing all that is the most freeing thing I have ever done!"

Lee whistles long and slow. "Well, she's a right little believer, Miss Maria."

Maria is smiling. "And rightly so. We need a lot more like Rosa in this world."

"To plough the fields?"

"To pray for you, Lee van Der Berg."

Lee laughs loudly.

Nina, with her two children, appear

across the street. She is shaking Liesbeth violently and screaming at her. The nuns turn to look. A Villager chastises Nina for mistreating Liesbeth.

"Who is that, Lee?"

"Nina Hager. A bit of a wild one. She's had her share of trouble."

"She's not coping with her children, is she? What does her husband do?

"She's not married."

"Is she a woman of easy virtue?"

"In this village??? No-one has any money. She struggles to put food on the table."

"No regular man in her life?"

"Old man Gutten's son, Christien. They've been on and off since they were fourteen."

"Are they his children?"

"She claims they are his."

"Is it true?"

"Maybe, maybe not. Gutten's father is a wealthy man. She might just see him as her meal ticket for her kids."

The distant TOLL of the convent bell. Juliana and Rosa are unloading the bicycles. Juliana interrupts Maria's conversation with Lee.

"Prayers, sister." Juliana mounts her

bike. Rosa pushes her bike towards Maria.

"Come along, sister."

Maria shakes Lee's hand. "Goodbye, Mister Van der Berg." Maria mounts the saddle behind Rosa. She is unable to peddle because of her bad leg. Rosa pushes off. They wobble at first, straighten.

"I'll come out and mend the tractor. No charge."

"Thank you, Lee."

"Good day, sisters."

The three nuns on the two bicycles head out of the village.

*

In the Abbess's room, Agnes is on her knees praying. A single KNOCK on her door. Agnes breaks from her prayers.

"Come!" Lucia and Heleen enter. Agnes is now on her feet. "I was just reminding myself of the twelve steps. Shall we recite them together?"

"As you wish."

All three recite the order's guiding rules. "Fear God; Substitute one's will to the will of God; Be obedient to one's superior; Be patient amid hardships; Confess one's sins; Accept oneself as a "worthless workman"; Consider oneself "inferior to all"; Follow examples set by superiors; Do not speak until spoken to; Do not laugh; Speak simply and modestly; Be humble in bodily posture. Amen."

Agnes leans forward, lights a candle. "In the old days, a candle burnt in the dormitory throughout the night. Now we have electric lights. Its not quite the same. They say they are ecological and economic. What could be more ecological or economic than a candle?"

Lucia nods, then hesitantly speaks.

"Mother Superior. We wish to call a council."

"Over this slur? We have made our enquires and found nothing."

"Things are not well in this house." Lucia looks to Heleen for support. Heleen speaks boldly. "The rules are not being enforced, Mother. Disobedience, laughter and false modesty is rife."

Lucia's voice is commanding. "Sister Heleen and I wish you to step down as Mother Superior."

Agnes takes in the information

without any malice. "You want me to take a pilgrimage like my predecessor?"

Lucia is callous. "It is inevitable, is it not?"

A look of relief wells in Agnes's face. She sighs. "I have failed you. I know this in myself. From the beginning, I never wanted the responsibility ... it has been a penance rather than a privilege to be Abbess. I will be relieved to hand over to someone more able to put right the wrongs in this house."

Lucia and Heleen lower their heads in reverence. "Thank you, Mother."

Agnes sizes them up. She is still in charge and has her own observations to make about them.

"I am not the only one at fault. You have also failed as Prioress and Porter. The fear of God has been absent for some time. Laughter. False modesty. You should be admonished for allowing a relaxation of the rules. You have been truly worthless workmen."

"Agnes, please ....."

"Do not Agnes me!" She looks sternly into the faces of Lucia and Heleen. "I see it clearly now. You have been paying lip service to the rules of Benedict, circumventing them when it suits you. None of you are humble, none of you accept that you are inferior to each other, none of you fear God!" She bangs her hand on her desk. "Very well, I agree to stand down as Mother Superior ..."

Lucia has won. She hides her glee. "You will oversee the council and the election?"

"Of course. You must have a true spouse of Christ to lead this house in a life of prayer, reading and manual work. Only then will I be able leave you to make my pilgrimage as you suggest."

Heleen is bubbling with the success of her plan. "Wise and practical, Mother Superior."

Agnes turns her attention to Heleen. "As no doubt you are behind these changes, do you have a list of possible candidates?"

Heleen is cautious. "No, Mother, we wanted to have your blessing first."

Agnes steps back. She has uncovered the ambition of the two plotters who are getting rid of her. "Notify the community that we require nominations. You may go, Heleen."

"Thank you, Mother." Heleen leaves.

Agnes sits in her chair. "Of course, Lucia, I cannot allow you to be put forward as the new abbess."

"Mother ....?"

"You are too ambitious. Being a sister is not a career. It is a conversion to a life of poverty and celibacy."

Lucia hides her disappointment. "Thank you, Mother."

"For what. Saving you from yourself? You are not liked by the sisters, you must work harder on your humility. You have a bold posture but you are not humble. Pride is the precipice to eternal damnation."

"Yes, Mother. My pride eats at me. It was my upbringing."

"Leave that baggage behind you. You are an excellent Prioress, but the new abbess has the right to replace you. Only God knows if that will be the best thing for our community."

Agnes gets up and compassionately lays her hand on Lucia's sleeve. "We are old friends, Lucia. Our love for one another once knew no bounds. Responsibility has kept us apart. We are now about to be set free."

Agnes kisses Lucia on the cheek. Lucia's frosty exterior dissolves. She puts her arms around Agnes and places her head on Agnes's shoulder.

*

Juliana, Humbelina and Idesbalda in muslin nightdresses are huddled together on a bed. Petra shoves in.

"What are you up to?"

Humbelina puts aside her irritation.

"Making a list of who we might like to be the new Abbess." She shows Petra the list.

"There's only one name here????"

Juliana snatches back the list.

"Exactly."

In another part of the dormitory. Roberta and Alberica are on their beds, still in their tunics, lying prostrate on their fronts. Alberica is moaning. Roberta is asleep. Blood is dripping from Alberica's bed on to the floor. Alberica's groans are being ignored.

Petra is adamant. "She won't do it."

Juliana is dismissive. "If she's

elected, she doesn't have any choice."

"What about Heleen?" Petra's suggestion is met with guffs. Idesbalda is curt.

"Do you like Heleen?"

Petra shakes her head. "I see what you mean. There must be somebody else?"

Humbelina offers up "Harindis?"

Petra is in two minds. "Alright. Put her down."

Humbelina scribbles on the paper. Idebalda whispers. "How about Alberica?" They all snigger.

Juliana looks across the dormitory. "She's daft about Roberta. They'd be inseparable. We'd have two abbesses." They all snigger again. Alberica groans loudly. They put their hands over their mouths, stifle their laughter.

"Its between these two then .... there's enough of us to swing the vote either way."

Maria and Lutgard enter with books under their arms. The nuns disperse to their own beds. Lutgard senses something is going on. Humbelina's bed is next to Lutgard's.

"What are you all up to?"

"We thought that Harlindis would make a good Abbess?

Maria overhears the remark. "I'd be up for voting for her. She's sensible, reliable and a good listener." Maria prepares to get into her bed which is next to Petra's.

"You not interested in being the Abbess, Maria?"

She keeps her back turned to Petra.

"Heavens, no. All that responsibility, keeping everyone in line, giving moral guidance, leading Our Lady of Rome procession into the village every year. Definitely not."

Harlindis with a towel over her shoulder comes in from the bathroom. The others say nothing to her. Lutgard sits down on the end of Maria's bed.

"Think of all the perks. Your own room to sleep. Your own room to pray. The opportunity to go on pilgrimages."

"I don't want to go anywhere. I'm quite happy, thank you. I like my life as it is. Modest and simple. I pray, I read, I work in the fields. What more could a sister ask for?"

Alberica is still groaning.

Maria is concerned. "Alberica? Do

you need help to undress?"

The other sisters exchange knowing looks.

"Turn the light on, Rosa."

Rosa gets up, switches on a small electric lamp. Maria gets down on her knees by Alberica's bed. "Don't despair, sister. Think of Christ's suffering on the way to the cross."

Alberica opens her eyes. "Is Roberta alright?"

"She's sleeping." Maria covers Alberica with a blanket, makes a short prayer. She rises, gets into bed. Rosa throws the light switch plunges the dormitory into darkness.

5

Idesbalda is pulling loaves from the bakery oven. Christien, looking mischievous, creeps up on her and slaps her on the bum. The tray clatters to the floor.

"Let me help you, sister." Ideabalda blushes in embarrassment. Christien replaces the contents on the tray.

"There we are."

"You're not supposed to be in here?"

"I'm not doing any harm. I'm looking for Sister Harlindis?"

"She's reading scriptures."

"How about Sister Maria then? I've a load of flour to be paid for."

Idesbalda wipes her hands, indicates to him to wait outside.

*

Christien is leaning against a wall smoking a near finished cigarette. Maria arrives out of the bakery.

"You took your time?"

"I was in the chapel."

"How are you?"

"Well enough. Can I help you?"

Christien hands her a delivery note.

"I put the bags in the storage unit."

Maria looks at the bill, frowns.

"If its too much, I can get the money another time."

"I don't think there should be another time."

"Have I done something wrong?"

Roberta and Alberica appear pushing a bakery rack. They are sullen and in obvious pain.

"Sister Roberta. Can you go to the unit and check off this delivery, please."

"Gladly, sister."

She abandons the rack, takes the paper from Maria. Roberta walks off slowly, shadowed by Alberica. Maria takes out a purse from her tunic,counts out a number of notes, gives them to Christien.

"That's all I have for you today, Mister Guttens."

"Thank you, sister. No time for a chat then?"

Maria ignores him, pushes the rack into the bakery. Christien pockets the notes and goes.

*

Lutgard, Petra, Harlindis are making last minute preparations in the hall.

The bell TOLLS. The sisters make way and stand at the side of the room - the rest of the community of Sisters filter through assorted doors. There are soft whispers of excitement. Heleen enters - claps her hands. The community falls silent. Agnes enters followed by Lucia. Heleen claps her hands again. The Nuns seat themselves. Lutgard, Petra and Harlindis join them. Agnes stands alone on the dais.

"Sisters. First may I say I am humbled to have guided you for the last seven years. As a community we have experienced hardship in these difficult times. However, I like to think that we thrive on hardship. Blessed is the Lord.

The nuns rejoice. "Blessed is the Lord!

"We are a school for the Lord's service. He is our salvation. Through patience we will share in the passion of Christ and his Kingdom. Blessed is the Lord.

The nuns repeat. "Blessed is the Lord."

Agnes takes out a piece of paper, unfolds it. "You must choose another Abbess, a new Mother Superior to guide you towards salvation. As a community you must choose wisely, indeed, ponder deeply before making your decision. God is watching us, Christ is with us." Agnes hands the paper to Lucia. "You have shortlisted two nominations and each will now be asked to say some words to us." Agnes seats herself.

Lucia stands up. "Sister Heleen ....."

Heleen is partly surprised, pleased. The Sisters clap gently as she steps on to the dais and faces the community.

"Thank you, sisters. We have been guided by our Mother Superior for seven years and I am in awe of the kindness, humility and charity she has extended to us. As Mother Superior, I would return us to our fundamental values of self discipline, restrict visits to the village, and implement immediate punishments for any break of the Order's rules. We are here to experience and share in our Lord's suffering, not to laugh and joke and have an easy life. We must curb our excesses, guard against sloth in our thinking, pray more, read more, work harder in our manual tasks, and regain our purpose ... a life of martyrdom and service to the true king, our Lord Jesus Christ." Heleen moves to the side of the dais. There is some polite clapping.

Lucia stands up once more. "Sister Maria ...." There is enthusiastic clapping. Maria is openly shocked when she hears her name. She looks to Harlindis. Harlindis motions her to stand up.

"Sister Maria .... will you come up and address us, please." Maria is reluctant. Humbelina tries to force her to stand. "Sister, you must speak to us!" Lucia's patience is wearing thin. Maria stumbles forward, mounts the dais.

"I cannot guide you, sisters. There is sin in me. Pride, lust, envy. I fear I will fan these sins with wrath instead of dowsing them with patience." She hesitates. "I eat too much at supper, I get depressed easily when it rains, I talk more than I listen. Its better by far we are guided by Sister Heleen." Maria hops awkward from one foot to the other.

Lucia calls up to her. "Is that all, sister?"

"Yes, sister. Please everyone,

choose sister Heleen" Maria shuffles back to her seat.

Agnes stands up.

"The matter is in your hands. Please deliberate freely and discuss wisely. It is your community. You will be asked to cast your votes at the next council meeting one week from today. Sister Lucia will keep you informed. Praise be to God."

All assembled. "Praise be to God!"

*

In the chapel a small group of Sisters facing one another are singing Ave Maria. The singing rises into the rafters.

Outside, going away from the Abbey, Rosa, with Maria on the back, is bicycling towards the village. "Why don't you want to be Mother Superior, Maria?"

"I am not fit to lead the community, Rosa. Harlindis is a much better choice. She should have ben shortlisted."

"I don't think so. We all love you."

"Love can be blind."

Rosa is waiting outside the chemist

shop with the bicycle. She is curious about the Passers-by. They are courteous to her. Maria emerges from the shop.

"You have the ointment?"

Maria nods, hands her a bandage and a tin of ointment. Rosa puts the items in the bicycle basket. Maria looks across the street. Karl catches her eye. Waves. Maria waves back, mounts behind Rosa.

They cycle out of the village.

*

Inside the bakery, Idesbalda, is sitting in tears. Lutgard is bandaging her outstretched arm. Maria and Rosa stand by.

"Its easily done, Idesbalda. I've burnt myself countless times taking the bread out of the oven.

"It was Christien Guttens fault. He was ... here again, Lutgard. He laid his hands on me.

"Why would he touch you?"

Maria gives a quick reply. "Because he used to be a priest."

Lutgard's face expresses what she thinks of priests. "That explains his wandering hands. Lucky you, Idesbalda."

"He was looking for Maria!"
Lutgard's eyes narrow suspiciously.
"He wants paid for the last delivery."
"I thought you had paid him?"
Idesbalda is in pain.
"Not the full amount ....."
Lutgard detects something is amiss.
She continues to wrap Idesbalda's
arm. She is direct with Maria. "Could
you tell him to stay out of the
bakery. Its ... unhygienic. Not
healthy."
"You are quite right." Maria gives
Lutgard a smile. Lutgard knows that
Maria is holding something back.

*

The Sisters are eating their evening
meal in the refectory. Juliana is
reading from the *Imitation of Christ*.
Humbelina is picking at her plate.
She looks pale. Maria signals across
the table to Harlindis. Suddenly,
Humbelina rolls backwards and
collapses on the floor. Juliana stops
reading.
Harlindis is first to help her.
"Humbelina, you silly girl. You have
to start eating chicken and fish."
"I don't want to eat God's creatures.
I'd rather die."

"You will die if you don't."
There is blood on Harlindis's hand. The back of Humbelina's tunic is soaked in blood. Their eyes meet but nothing is said. Harlindis helps Humbelina out of the refectory. Juliana begins reading again. The Sisters recommence eating in silence.

*

The library is silent. Maria, Lutgard, Petra, Harlindis, Idesbalda are reading in complete silence except for the sound of turning pages.

*

It is a bright sunny day. The Sisters are working in a field with Karl who is helping them to attach a trailer to the tractor.
"Your wife is better, Karl?"
"So, so. The doctors don't know what's wrong with her. She gets fevers in the night.
"How old is she?"
"Forty two. Her mother died at that age. It worries me."
"People live longer nowadays. The advances are incredible. Life-span has been increasing by two years a

decade for the last fifty years.

"Is that a fact. How old are you Maria?

"I'm thirty four."

"How long have you been .....?"

"Fourteen years."

"What did you do before that?"

"I was going to study to be a lawyer."

"A lawyer! I read somewhere that they are the most selfish people in the world."

"I can believe that."

"Not for you then?"

"No. At university I was searching for a relationship. I found it in God."

"What did your parents think?"

"They were dismayed."

"And now?"

"My mother has accepted my choice, my father ... he still hopes I will wake up from my dream and return to my real family. He says I am wrong to have rejected them for the poverty of religious fundamentalism. He doesn't understand. All I want is a simple life. I have no desire for possessions and modern comforts."

"Do you know what the villagers call you?"

"No, but I'm interested."

"Blackbirds."

Maria smiles. "That's not so bad. I've heard most terms shouted at me … crows, bats, penguins. Blackbirds I like. They sing in the morning, are industrious all day, and then sing again at night. It describes us perfectly. I can't take offence at that."

Karl admires Maria. "You are one of a kind, Sister Maria. One of a kind!"

Maria blushes.

*

It is early evening. Lurgard is in the abbey garden. There is the sound of singing from the chapel. She is smoking a cigarette. She is enjoying every draw she makes.

The sound of a lorry approaching. The faint hint of a headlight. Lutgard stares into the dark. The engine is switched off. Lutgard curious, stubs out her cigarette.

Lutgard approaches the farm barn. The singing is still heard faintly in the distance. There are VOICES from inside the barn. Lutgard goes to the barn door - listens - slips inside.

She moves silently towards the back of the barn. There are muted grunts and groans. She steps forward - instantly pulls back.

Christien is standing with his trousers around his ankles - his buttocks bare, clenching and unclenching slowly.

Lutgard strains to see more clearly. His hands are on the bare breasts of a whimpering woman bent in front of him. A nun's tunic lies discarded on the barn floor.

Lutgard tries frantically to see who it is. Christien pulls away, roughly turns the naked woman to face him.

He pushes her backwards into the straw without revealing her face. The woman's legs are splayed out by him.

Lutgard gives out a gasp. One of the legs is calipered. As he thrusts at her, the woman's face is revealed.

It is Maria!

Lutgard rushes out.

Back in the abbey garden, the singing has stopped. Lutgard is chain smoking. She is an emotional wreck. She cocks an ear. The sound of a lorry driving off. Maria comes out of the dark, almost bumps into Lutgard.

"Lutgard! You scared the life out of me."

Lutgard lights up another cigarette.

"Those things will kill you." Maria takes a ciggy from her.

"Out for a walk?"

"Its a fresh night ..."

"Very fresh ....."

"Have I done something wrong?"

"You tell me?"

A look passes between them that cuts through the lies.

"I've had it with this place. I'm going to leave at the end of the month."

"Lutgard, you can't. You've left twice before. A third time and you can never come back."

"Come back to what? Hypocrisy? This place is a joke."

Lutgard turns quickly, speeds off. Maria puts her head in her hands.

*

Maria is showering alone. She is trying to cleanse herself, continually scrubbing herself, repeatedly, over and over.

She breaks down and cries.

*

In the Abbess's room, Maria is kneeling before Agnes washing her feet.

"You are my preferred choice, Maria. Sister Heleen is too under the influence of Sister Lucia. The community needs someone like you to fire them up, someone to stop them acting like old maids and spinsters."

"Yes, Mother Superior." Maria reaches for a small towel.

"Get up, daughter! I can still bend to dry my own feet."

Maria gets up, hands Agnes the towel.

"Now, I want an answer. Are you ready to guide the Sisters?

"I have grave doubts, Mother Superior."

"And so you should."

"I know that I am not worthy."

Agnes looks into Maria's eyes. "I'm listening ...."

Maria is on the verge of revealing her secret. Something stops her.

"Come, tell me ...."

"Sister Lutgard wants to leave the convent." She has passed the point of honesty.

"Go on, child ....."

"I have not been a good friend to Lutgard. When she returned the last time, I promised the Lord that I would be her truest friend and devote myself to her salvation. I have broken my promise with God. I have thought only about myself and abandoned Lutgard."

"Lutgard is the concern of us all, Maria. She struggles with her thoughts of lust and envy, she has told me so. The temptations of the outside world are just too great for her."

"Yes, Mother, but she is a good soul. I have tried to be an example to her, but I have failed."

"Nonsense, Maria. She has told me how much you are responsible for her return. It was you she thought about every day. It was because of you she returned."

"I've failed her, Mother."

"Stop this now. Both times she has left here, she has fallen in with men. I have always suspected Lutgard capable of doing that here."

"No, Mother, I don't believe that."

"I think she is the guilty one."

Maria turns away in shame.

"Come, Maria, you expect too much from everyone." She takes her and comforts her. "Whether the woman's accusation was prompted by fact or envy, it is better that Lutgard leaves of her own will. The matter will close with her."

Maria looks at Agnes, disappointed with her judgment of Lutgard. "What if it is not Lutgard?"

"That will be something for the new Mother Superior to deal with."

6

The community has gathered in the refectory to cast their votes. A large wooden box is being passed around. The nuns are slipping their ballot papers into the box. Lutgard, hesitant, looks to Maria. Maria exchanges the long look. Lutgard drops her ballot into the box. Maria looks at her own ballot sheet. Two names - Sister Heleen and Sister Maria. Maria puts her mark for Sister Heleen, folds her paper, puts it in the box. She turns and smiles to Heleen. Heleen smiles back.

*

Maria, Lutgard, Petra, Juliana and Harlindis are tidying up with brooms and shovels. Juliana is beaming at Maria. "Aren't you excited, Maria?"
"About what?"
"Finding out if you are the new Abbess."
Lutgard throws down her shovel, walks off a little, lights a cigarette.
"I hope everyone has been sensible enough to select Heleen."
Juliana stops sweeping. "I voted for you."

Harlindis adds her voice. "Me too. Petra?" Petra says nothing. "Petra????"

"It was a secret ballot. I prefer to keep it secret."

Sister Lucia approaches. Lutgard stubs out her cigarette. "Sister Lutgard. Can you come with me please."

"Come where, sister?"

Lucia turns her anger on her. "You are an insolent malcontent, Lutgard Smeets. As long as you are here with us, you will be obedient. Give me that packet of cigarettes!"

Lutgard hands over the packet. Lucia stuffs them in her tunic and glares at the other sisters.

"Get on with your labours!" Turns to Lutgard. "Follow me." Lucia trots off with Lutgard not far behind.

Petra is sneering. "She is just sick with power. Imagine her as Mother Superior?"

Harlindis "Will she still be the Prioress after the election?"

"That's up to the new Mother." Petra throws Maria a questioning look. Maria turns and carries on with her work.

Juliana pulls out a packet of

cigarettes from her pocket. Hands them around. "Lutgard wants to leave again."

Petra lights up. "Every time she leaves, she's back within a month. She's not made for the outside world. Now, Maria, she'd cope where ever she went."

Maria straightens up. "What makes you say that, Petra?"

"Its true isn't it?"

Juliana exhales. "I don't think so. Maria is a saint. She would get angry at all the injustices out there."

"That is exactly right. It would test my faith to the limit."

Petra sticks her tongue in her cheek. "Perhaps you wouldn't need Christ in the outside world."

"Sister Petra!" Juliana is angry.

"It's alright, Juliana. Petra is just testing me."

"Well? Would you?"

"You are right, Petra. If I lived in the outside world I would not need Jesus for my salvation. I would miss his companionship. I would not be able to serve him as I do here."

"That's because the world is a busy place ...."

"Correct, Juliana. The need to make

a living, pay rent, put food on the table ... it would leave little time for praying and reading."

"It would be all hard labour to pay the overheads and taxes." Juliana is looking for reassurance. "Isn't that right?"

Harlindis stubs out her cigarette. "I wouldn't want that sort of life."

"Amen" replies Juliana.

The rest all mutter "Amen" and go back to work.

*

The sound of the running showers. In the changing room, Maria is putting on her tunic, Lutgard her scapula. There are marks on Lutgard's arms.

"Did the Prioress beat you?"

"She tried to shame me into leaving."

"You've done nothing wrong."

"Don't worry, she got nothing out of me."

Maria averts her eyes.

"Look, Maria, its not working out for me here. I just need another couple of weeks to get things arranged on the outside."

"I'm not going to give up on you."

"You already have, Maria. I thought you were as pure as snow. How wrong I was."

"I'm far from perfect, Lutgard."

"I see that now. You're quite a selfish little bitch, arn't you. Are you going to accept?"

"What?

"When they make you the Abbess."

"Its not even a possibility."

"Is that the saintly Maria speaking."

Maria blushes.

"God help us if they have picked you."

*

In the refectory the Sisters are eating without speaking. Harlindis reads from the scriptures.

*

In the great hall the room has been set for the inauguration of the new Abbess. There is a low expectant murmur from the nuns on the benches.

Heleen and Maria stand on the dais with Agnes and Lucia who opens the procedings. "Sisters. You have chosen a new Abbess. Before we ask her to take her place as our new

Mother Superior, we must thank Sister Agnes for a few parting words." The Sisters break into spontaneous polite applause. Agnes holds up her hand.

"The reunification of one's own will and the arming of one's self with the weapons of obedience under the banner of Christ our Lord is why we are here. My successor has been chosen by you for her charity, temperance, diligence and kindness. With patience, humility and chastity, she will guide you. But above all else, she has been chosen because she does not want to be Mother Superior." An exited murmur breaks out. Agnes quells it with a raised hand. "The new Abbess believes she is not worthy, because she struggles to keep her promises with God. We can all identify with that."

There is a terrified look of anguish on Maria's face throughout the speech. "Your new Abbess is Sister Maria."

Maria is visibly ashen. The Sisters break into a joyous clapping. A disappointed Heleen leads Maria towards Agnes. A bowl of water is placed at Maria's feet. Agnes kneels down and begins to wash Maria's feet. Maria is bewildered.

Lucia surveys the rapturous community of nuns. Lutgard is the only one not clapping. She looks from Lutgard to Maria and back again. Juliana nudges Lutgard to clap. Lutgard ignores her.

Maria holds up her hand. The clapping stops instantly. Maria helps Agnes up from the floor.

"Sister Humbelina, please. Everyone else, please return to your duties." Maria claps her hands twice to signal the gathering is over. The Sisters disperse. Humbelina mounts the dais.

"Can you help Sister Agnes to move to her new cell."

Humbelina is beaming with joy. "Yes, Mother Superior."

They depart.

"Prioress. Can you call Sister Petra and Sister Lutgard to my study."

Lucia is struggling to suppress her contempt for Maria. She exchanges glances with Heleen.

"Yes, Mother Superior." The words are soaked with bitterness.

*

In the Abbess's room, the sound of chapel singing invades the walls. Maria, dressed now as Mother Superior, is examining her new surroundings. There is a KNOCK

"Come!" Petra and Lutgard enter followed by Lucia and Heleen.

"Sisters .... let's get down to business. I am making changes to how matters are organised. Sister Petra. You will be our new Prioress."

Petra is astounded, but as pleased as punch. Lucia is wounded.

"You have been taxed by the duties of Porter, Heleen. You will now have more time for prayer and reading."

Heleen appears to be relieved.

"Sister Lutgard will be our new Porter."

Lucia cannot contain herself. "This is outrageous!"

Lutgard is amused. "I agree."

Maria claps her hands. "I will have obedience. You may go Sister Lucia. Sister Heleen. Prioress. Can you help them to move to the dormitory."

Petra is grinning from ear to ear. "Sisters ....."

Petra leads Lucia and Heleen out. The door closes.

"I need you, Lutgard."

"I'm not going to take your confession."

"What do you mean?

"I saw you."

"Saw what?"

"You, with him!" Maria falls silent. "Well? Aren't you going to talk your way out of it?"

"Is this a confession?"

"Confession???? How are you going to absolve it?" Maria is shame faced. "You can't." She takes off her scapula. "I've packed my bags. I'm leaving tomorrow and you are leaving with me."

Maria is filled with fear. "I can't do that. I'm the Mother Superior."

"You are a sham. How long have I known you. Eight years? In that time I've been with two men. How many have you had?"

Maria slaps Lutgard hard across the face. She reels against the wall. "Thank you, Mother Superior." Lutgard walks boldly to the door, opens it. She leaves without a backward glance.

Maria slumps at her desk.

*

The door of the convent creaks open. Lutgard appears in modern clothing with a small bag in her hand. Harlindis steps out - hugs Lutgard - steps back inside. The door closes behind her.

Lutgard starts walking along the deserted country road towards the village.

Maria watches from a window.

*

Inside one of the village bars, Lutgard is sitting. She is heavily made up with mascara and lipstick.

She downs her third shot. Christien slides up next to her.

"Do I know you? I've seen you before."

"I've seen a lot more of you than you've seen of me." She laughs drunkenly. Christien points his finger, waves it at her.

"Sister Lutgard ....."

"That's me. No, sorry, that was me. My real name is Barbara Smeets. Ordinary girl, no fixed abode, looking for a job and a place to stay."

Christien eyes her up. "You want another drink, Barbara?"

"I don't mind if I do. Can you make it a double?"

*

Idesbalda's arm is now only partial bandaged. Lucia is helping her to remove a tray from the bakery oven.
"You enjoy this work, Sister Lucia?"
"No, I do not."
Idesbalda is obviously not liking working with her either. "Why don't you try the farm. They are short handed without Sister Lutgard."
"I will learn to serve Christ our Lord by your side, sister."
"Suit yourself, sister." She makes a face to Roberta and Alberica.   They giggle.

*

Lutgard is face down naked on the bed. She is totally submissive. There are fresh red stripe marks across her back. Christien is removing his trousers.
"Get on your hands and knees." She does as she is told, arches herself up on to her knees. He crouches behind her. Her right hand clutches a small wooden cross. As he enters

her - her fingers increasingly tighten around the cross.

*

In the abbey chapel, the Sisters are singing their praises to Christ, the Lord.

*

In the hotel room, Christien wrenches the cross from Lutgard's hand, throws it on the floor.

*

The Sisters are working in the fields. They are still singing.

*

In the hotel room, Christien is now on his back. Lutgard is lying on her back on top of him. The fingers of one hand are in her mouth, his other hand clutching at her groin. Lutgard is arching and stretching her arms out (as if on a cross) as he takes her from below.

*

The Sisters are in the showers. They are joyful and playful.

*

In the hotel room, Christien buttons up his pants. Lutgard lies naked and used on the bed. Her mascara has run and her lipstick is smeared across her face. Christien digs into his pocket, pulls out some notes, throws them on to the bed.

"You'll soon learn to pay your way, Barbara." Lutgard doesn't even turn to look at him. He picks up his shirt, throws it on, leaves. Lutgard reaches for the cross on the floor, grips it tightly.

*

Maria is alone in the abbey office sewing the hem of a scapula. The telephone rings. She stops sewing, picks up the receiver.

"Mr. Koeken at the village hotel? Barbara Smeets? Yes, that's Sister Lutgard ...."

Maria drops the receiver out of her hand.

*

In the hotel room, the dangling legs of Lutgard. She has hanged herself.

7

The abbey graveyard. Tolling BELLS. The Sisters file out of the cemetery behind two robed priests, Father Armand and Father Bernard. Karl stops Maria as she exits the cemetery gate.

"I didn't know you could provide salvation for someone who committed suicide?"

Maria is circumspect. "By ways known to him alone, God can provide the opportunity for repentance. These days the Church prays for persons who have taken their own lives."

"She must have been severely disturbed?"

"Suffering, or torture can diminish the responsibility of anyone."

The two Priests are laughing, joking with some of the Sisters. They are showing Rosa more attention than the others.

"Torture?"

"Mental torture, Karl. No single sin, not even suicide, evicts a person from heaven into hell."

"But what caused her to hang herself?"

"I want to believe that Lutgard finally gave up her resistance and accepted the forgiveness of Christ.

"She was seen with Christien Guttens before she died?" Maria is visibly disturbed by this news. "This might shock you, Maria, but for ages there were rumours about him going up to your farm and having sex with her."

Petra and Juliana approach with Harlindis

"My condolences, sisters" Karl slips off.

"Maria ..." Harlindis is hesitant "Father Armand and Father Bernard want to come to the convent for coffee."

Maria is adamant. "No! As Porter, tell them one of our sisters has measles and you can't admit them."

Harlindis is relieved. She trots back to the Priests. Maria watches as Harlindis speaks to the Priests. They start to raise their voices in anger. Harlindis points to Maria who puts her hands together as if in prayer. Bernard returns the gesture, turns Armand towards their parked car.

The majority of Sisters are well

ahead of Maria, Petra and Juliana as they walk up the road towards the abbey.

"That closes a chapter."

"Show some charity, Petra. You must pray for her."

Petra reflects. "Forgive me. I often clashed with Lutgard. It was wrong of me. She will be in my evening prayers."

"But for the grace of God go us."

"That's an odd thing to say, Mother Superior" Juliana exclaims.

"We are all sinners, Juliana, with our lusting mortal flesh."

Petra wipes her hands on her tunic. "I'll have no more lust near my flesh. I've had past humiliations at the hands of filthy priests. I was twelve when I entered a convent." They continue to walk. "As a novice, I never met a priest who had not been drinking. I was too scared to fight any of them off. I was helpless, they did to me whatever invention their depraved minds could come up with. I think every bride of Christ has gone through that."

Juliana turns away and bursts into tears.

"Juliana?" Maria comforts Juliana.

"Its time we talked to each other about this instead of God."

Juliana is angered by what she has heard. "That's slothful thinking, Maria! I've sacrificed everything to pray for lost humanity. You can't tell me it has all been for nothing!"

"We are like sheep led to slaughter. Did the Holy Ghost place the seed in the Virgin Mary's womb? Because a priest represents the Holy Ghost, is it alright for us to bear priests children?" Juliana thoughts are scrambled by Maria's words.

Maria utters the words they have never dared speak before "We get rid of them, don't we?

Juliana is close to tears "Yes ....."

"Its not right, is it?"

"No."

"And the Pope knows it goes on in convents around the world."

Juliana bursts into uncontrollable sobbing. "They took the little thing from me and smothered it!"

Petra takes Juliana in her arms. Maria is upset by Juliana's breakdown. Petra is strong.

"You too, Maria?"

"Twice."

"Four times for me."

They stand in the road motionless come to terms with their collective grief.

*

Christien arrives in his van with a supply of flour. Christien appears in the bakery doorway. Idesbalda shouts at him.

"You've to clear off!"

"Don't talk to me like that! Where's Sister Maria?"

"She's Mother Superior now. Go on, clear off! You've to stay out of the here."

Christien holds up a delivery note.

"Somebody has to pay for this. Does she still pay the bills?"

"Sister Juliana deals with that now. Alberica! Fetch Juliana!"

Alberica runs off. Christien laughs, comes straight up to Idesbalda. "I'd still prefer to see the Mother Superior."

He pushes past Idesbalda.

*

Maria is in the chapel on her knees praying. There is the sound of VOICES. Maria opens her eyes. Christien appears in the chapel followed by a protesting Juliana. Maria gets on her feet.

"He will only speak with you, Maria."

"That's fine, Juliana. You may go."

Juliana reluctantly leaves. Christien wanders further into the chapel, looks upwards.

"You feel safe in here?"

"What sort of man are you?"

"I'm just an ordinary working fellow."

"Were you responsible for Lutgard's death?"

"I wanted to speak to you about that."

"Were you responsible?"

"No, I was not. She was perfectly fine when I left her."

"So you were with her the night she died."

"Only until early evening. We had a couple of drinks. She wasn't a nun no more, was she? I told the police all that."

"You could have helped her?"

"Tried to. She said you two had a bust up and she'd left the convent. She didn't have much money, none of you lot do." He waves his delivery note. "I got her fixed up with the hotel room for the night."

"That was kind of you. Did you do anything else for her?"

"Listened to her crying. She wasn't the happiest rabbit on the planet. When I left her she was a bit miserable. We didn't talk much so I didn't know that she was going to do that to herself."

Maria is put off her guard, lets Christien move closer to her.

"So you're the top bitch now?"

"That's foul thinking."

"Sorry, you know I'm not in robes anymore, but after the things we've done, bitch seems the right word."

"I'll not have you speak to me like that."

Christien is moving closer to her. "How do you want me to speak to you? All lovey dovey like one of the choir singers?" Christien is within an arm's reach of her. "Mother Superior. Who would have thought it. A dirty little whore like you becoming the Abbess." Maria backs away. He catches hold of her, whispers in her ear. "I want you on your knees. Now!" Maria is terrified, she does as she is told. "Take off that thing!"

Maria unstraps her metal leg

support - discards it. "Now take off your clothes." Maria removes her scapula. He takes it from her, folds it neatly, places it on the altar. Maria is removing her tunic. It is halfway over her head. Christian pushes her backwards on to the altar steps, her arms trapped and her head covered by the tunic.

He forces her legs apart, drops on to her. Maria is in a panic, struggling to breathe. He pushes his way into her, pulls the tunic up over her head. "Are those old priests still doing you lot, eh? Dirty animals. Wiping their filthy hands on you, breathing their sinking fumes into your face." Maria is petrified. "Putting the fear of God into you. Quite right too. If Jesus won't come down and have you, then the priests might as well do it for him, eh?"

Maria is looking away to the image of Christ on the Cross above the altar. She closes her eyes. Christien slaps the side of her face. "No you don't. You keep those eyes open." Maria stares opened eyed straight at him. "That's my girl."

Roberta and Alberica appear hand in hand in the chapel aisle.

Christien half turns, shouts "Get out!" They run away.

He reaches into his pocket pulls out the delivery note. "You still got to pay this, right?" Maria nods her head. "I'm not hurting you enough, am I?" Maria shakes her head. She is beyond struggle. "Good ......"

He thrusts his hands around her throat, half strangles her, comes with a loud groan. Released from his grip, Maria gasps for breath, turns her head in shame. Christien gets up, straightens his clothes. "I'll go find Juliana." Maria grabs her tunic, covers herself.

"Oh just so you know, your dead friend, told me that she was in love with you. How's that possible, eh? You're all supposed to be in love with Jesus Christ?"

Christien leaves. Maria turns in her naked state, gets on her knees. "Forgive me! Forgive me! Forgive me!" The dead-eyed effigy of Christ stares down at her. She stares back, something in her mind, a thought, triggers her to slowly get to her feet. The dead eyed statutes in the chapel stare down at her. She beings to mumble to herself.

"Its a lie ..... you're all metal, wood and plaster. All the prayers poured out to you by faithful and deluded people all over the world. For what? For this?" She drops her tunic - leaves the chapel naked except for the cross around her neck.

*

Inside the bakery Idesbalda turns in disbelieve. Lucia does the same. Maria is limping through the bakery naked. She goes out the open door into the yard.

*

Humbelina is driving the tractor with Lee Van de Berg hanging off the side looking at the wheels. A look of horror crosses her face - and Lee's.
She stops the tractor dead. Maria is crossing the field naked. She falls on her knees into the dirt. Humbelina and Lee run towards her, reach her.
Lee takes off his jacket, throws it over her shoulders.
"You are not looking well, Mother Superior."
Maria rejects the jacket. "I am perfectly well. I'm doing penance. Please don't touch me." She

instructs Humbelina. "Get me some farm clothes." Humbelina does as she is told, runs off.

*

A pile of farm clothes hang on a peg. Maria is alone in the shower.
She is scrubbing herself vigorously, more so than the time before.

*

Maria is being sick in a small sink in her cell at the back of the office. There is a KNOCK. Maria straightens herself, comes out into the office. "Come!"
Juliana enters. "Are the sisters' monthly letters ready to post?"
"Yes."
"I'm excited about the procession to the village church tomorrow." Juliana looks at the letters on the desk, picks one up. "You haven't gone through them?"
"I've read them all."
"You haven't edited them?" She half jokes "You don't want their fathers' coming to take their daughters away?"
Maria goes to her desk, takes up an ink brush. "Which letter should I

start with?

Juliana picks out a letter. "Rosa's."

Maria looks at Rosa's letter. "What should I brush out?

"The reference to Father Bernard."

Maria re-looks at the letter. "When I first took orders, my letters from home were so brushed out there was virtually nothing left to read. I used to weep over all those inked out sections, wondering and worrying over what my mother had been trying to tell me."

"We can't allow certain things to become public."

"Are we a secret organisation?"

"We are part of the Roman Catholic Church."

"Why don't we have a single bible in the convent?"

"You know why. Its forbidden."

"Why? What's so wrong with reading the bible for ourselves?" Maria opens a drawer, pulls our a bible, opens it. Juliana's face turns red. She snatches the bible from Maria's hand, throws it to the floor. She slams her foot on the bible, spins around with all her weight, ripping it, breaking the binding."

"If you had put your foot on my

face, I doubt it would have hurt half as much as witnessing this." Maria picks up the destroyed book. "If priests had the power, they would go house-to-house, seize all the Bibles, soak them with gasoline and burn them all."

Maria takes another bible from the desk. "You cannot destroy the word of God by trampling on it. Priests cannot destroy us by trampling on us."

There is another KNOCK at the door. "Come!" Rosa enters, stands with downcast eyes.

"Take off your scapula.

Rosa removes her scapula. Maria pushes Rosa's tunic off her shoulders, pushes it down to her waist. There are huge deep welt marks on her back and across her breasts. Maria hands Rosa her letter, points to the part to read. "Read to us please."

Rosa is emotional "I was taken by Sister Lucia and Father Bernard to the basement where there was a large cross made of heavy timber, lying on its side. She stripped my clothes off down to the waist. Then she bent me down over the cross, pulled my hands below and fastened them securely to my knees."

"Go on, Rosa…."

"They began to flog me repeatedly with whips until my blood ran all over the floor."

There is another KNOCK.

Maria indicates Rosa to redress. "Come!" Harlindis enters with Petra.

"Pull up your tunic, Harlindis." Harlindis draws up her tunic to her waist. There a severe lacerations on her thighs. She motions her to turn around. The lacerations are also across her buttocks. Maria picks up a letter. "Tell us what you wrote about Father Armand. From this bit ... He took my confession. He was perched in a high chair ..."

Maria hands Harlindis her letter, but she doesn't need to read from it. "He ordered me to kneel between his legs. I wouldn't do what he wanted. So he kicked me to the floor, made me crawl up and down the aisle ten times, then lashed me with his studded belt. Then he sat down again, made me kneel between his legs ... and I did what he wanted." Maria motions Harlindis to cover herself.

"Standard treatment here, wouldn't you say?"

The nuns cast their eyes to the floor.

"Petra?"

Petra silently lets her tunic drop to the floor. Standing naked, we see her body has been badly scarred by burns.

"The sort of thing that the Mother Superior expunges with the stroke of a brush?"

Petra redresses. Maria walks to her desk, scoops up the letters.

"Send these as they are, Juliana."

"But Maria! ...." A look from Maria is enough to silence Juliana.

"Yes, Mother."

"It is time we came into the twentieth century."

8

The Sisters are sitting on the benches in the great hall. Maria is on the dais lecturing them.

"We all have scars. It has to stop. How did I get this bad leg? When I first joined the order, I was stung upside down in a dark cell by my thumbs and left hanging on my tip-toes. There I hung, wracked with pain and saturated in my own filth all day. On the wall there was an adjustable shelf raised to the level of my face. On it was a pan of water and a pan containing one small potato. I almost tore every tissue in my body to get to the water."

She pauses to let the story sink in.

"Ten days like that. I couldn't walk for two and a half months." Maria limps across the dais. "Christ was on the cross three days. We are told He received 667 strokes on His body; on His cheek 110 strokes; on His neck 107 strokes; on His back 180 strokes; on His breast 77 strokes; on His head 108 strokes; on His side 32 strokes. They spat in His face 32 times; threw Him to the ground 38 times. From the crown of thorns He received 100 wounds; pleaded for our salvation 900 times, and carried the cross 320 steps."

She hobbles as she talks.

"We're told that by experiencing suffering, we can understand what He suffered." Lucia cannot stand what she is hearing as Maria continues. "How is that possible. We are not the sons of God. We are mortals, good mortals, not creatures of sin. Christ died for our sins."

Lucia stands up. "Blasphemy!"

"Sit down, sister!" Lucia is pulled down by Haleen.

"Is that the kind of Mother Superior you want? Cruel, sadistic, heartless and evil. Those underground dungeons we have below where we have all been. Sister Lucia's domain is the dark torture chamber of Satan and his followers."

Lucia is angered beyond words. "This assembly is over!"

Maria is calm, knows her power. "Prioress ...."

Petra instructs some of the nuns to take hold of Lucia, drag her out. They take hold of Agness too, remove her from the hall. "Heleen ... " Agnes shouts. Heleen sits unmoved.

Harlindis and Rosa wheel in a trolley with two vegetable crates containing bibles. They start to hand out bibles. "Know Jesus for yourself, sisters."

*

Maria is walking with Karl in the abbey garden. "How can I terminate the service of Christien Guttens?"

"Very difficult. His father owns most of the land you farm."

"I though it belonged to the Abbey?"

"It did, but somehow old man Guttens did a deal with the Church during the war and bought it."

"What did the Church get in return?"

"His son. Except Christien left the priesthood over his affair with Nina Hager."

"He's still in love with her?"

"And her with him. They knock each other about. Its going to end with them killing one or the other."

Father Armand and Father Bernard are shown into the garden by Heleen. "This is all I need."

Father Armand is all smiles. "Goodday, Mother Superior. I've come about Sister Lucia."

Father Bernard pulls Karl aside, says

something to him. Karl is escorted by Bernard out of the garden.

Armand is overbearing "This is a convent, sister. I find you alone with a man. You are a disgrace to the Church." He grabs her by the arm.

"Unhand me ...."

"Cast down you eyes! I curse that they will rot and fall out of your head if you look at me again!" He hits her about the head. "You will obey me, woman, or may the maggots devour your organs." He knocks her to the ground.

Maria is defiant. "You may break every bone in my body, you cannot touch me."

"You are to reinstate Sister Lucia as Prioress. You hear! I want to see her leading the procession tomorrow!" Armand kicks her viciously, and repeatedly. "Sister Agnes is go on a pilgrimage! You will obey me!" Maria curls up into a ball. A hand pulls Armand back, a fist smashes into his face, knocks him over a wall. Karl picks Maria up.

"You mustn't help me!"

"I'm taking you to the police."

"No, you mustn't!"

Armand is on his feet.

"Clear off!" He pushes Armand again. Bernard emerges from a corner of the garden, helps Armand up. Armand and Bernard clear off.
"You don't know what you've done. They'll be back with six more priests. Ten. Twenty!"
"What is going on here?"

*

Karl is outside the front gate by his lorry. Maria, Petra and Juliana are inside the gate.
"You can't go ahead with the procession with all this going on?" Maria is silent but resolute. Karl looks up at the building. "This place is like a prison. If you can't get out, they can't get in. I'll be back in the morning with a reporter friend of mine from Antwerp."
Karl gets into his van.
They watch as he drives up the long road towards the village.

*

Locks are turned, the bolts are fastened, the doors are barred. Many of the Sisters are choir singing. Some of the Sisters are reading their bibles in the library.

Some Sisters are decorating a statue of the Virgin Mary with flowers.

Maria is nervously pacing the chapel aisle. Humbelina is speeding down the aisle towards her.
"Maria, you must come immediately!"

*

Humbelina leads Maria down the dark stairway and into the basement. At the bottom of the steps they are met by Idesbalda holding a candle. Idesbalda leads the way down a pitch black tunnel. At the end of the tunnel is a metal door with a grill. The face of Heleen appears. Maria is momentarily frightened. Heleen pushes open the cell door. Inside Petra is splattered in blood and holding a flagellater. Maria peers in to the gloom. Agnes, her head and wrists in a stock, is soaked in blood.
Petra is shaken. "I think she's dead."
Maria shakes her head. "Throw some water on her." Petra empties a bucket of water over Agnes. There is

a groan. "Release her and take her up to the dormitory."

*

Rosa removes the mattress from a bed. Idesbalda and Humbelina throw Agnes down on to the hard wooden boards. She screams in pain. Idesbalda has no compassion "Serves her right for all the times she ordered us to be chained up and flogged." They leave Agnes to her pain.

*

Back in the basement, another door is opened. Inside is Harlindis with a cat of six tails. Lucia is chained to the large wooden cross that Harlindis described to the others in the Abbess's room. Lucia's back is stripped of flesh and the floor is running with blood. Maria recoils, but only momentary.
"Have you shed enough blood for Christ our Lord, daughter?"
Lucia is broken. "I have, Mother, I have. Spare me, for the love of God, spare me!
On the floor is a plumber's blow torch. Maria indicates to Harlindis to

light it. The torch flares up the room. Maria stands over Lucia.

"Are you sorry for your wickedness, for standing up and disobeying me in front of the entire community?"

Lucia is repentant. "I'm truly sorry, Mother Superior, I'll never disobey you again. Never! Never! Never!"

"I don't believe you. You didn't believe any of us when we promised to obey the Mother Superior." Maria gives Harlindis the order to lower the burning torch on to Lucia's body. Lucia screams, bucks and pitches, wriggles in her attempts to escape the merciless fire on her back. Her clothing catches fire. She is writhing and shrieking in agony as her flesh sizzles.

Maria decides she has burned enough. Harlindis extinguishes the torch. They cover Lucia in a filthy rug to smother the flames. Lucia is like a wild creature, throbbing in white-hot pain and misery.

"We have bourne her cross, now its her turn to carry ours."

9

From the village end of the road, at a distance is an effigy of the Virgin Mary - carried in procession by the Sisters.

The small street to the local chapel is lined with Villagers. Lee van der Berg is in the crowd with his wife. There is a buzz of excitement. Father Bernard stands on the steps of the chapel looking down the street. He is apprehensive.

As the procession approaches, his face suddenly turns fully to anger. At the head of the procession is Maria holding aloft the Virgin on a pole. She is bare-breasted, her tunic free about her waist. Behind her, are the rest of the Sisters all bare breasted and bare-footed. At their centre is a bare-breasted Lucia hauling the large wooden cross. She is drenched in blood.

As the procession passes up the street, there is complete silence from the Villagers. The scars on the bodies of the nuns are plain for all to see.

Lucia stumbles. Roberta and Alberica whip her to her feet. The Villagers are in shock and awe at what they are witnessing.

As Maria approaches the steps of the chapel, Bernard descends to block her way. She pushes him aside and goes up the steps followed by Petra, Juliana and Harlindis.

Idesbalda and Humbelina free Lucia from the cross and carry her up the stairs. They are followed by the rest of the Sisters led by Heleen.

Father Armand is at the altar. In the front pew is Christien with his father Xavier Guttens. Beside them sits a demure Nina Hager. They entire congregation turns as Maria enters with the Virgin. There is a gasp as the bare-breasted nuns filter down the center aisle. The Villagers throng in behind the nuns. Father Bernard is swept up in the melee.

Armand strains to see who is carrying the Virgin, the light puts Maria in silhouette. Maria comes into the light, her bare breasts shocking everyone in the front row. Armand, seething in anger, descends from the altar, knocks the Virgin out of Maria's hands, floors her with a single stroke of his hand. The Virgin clatters to the floor, the ancient brittle relic splitting and breaking. The Congregation gasps.

Armand realises he has made a grave error. Maria picks herself up, Armand runs for the door behind the altar. The Congregation is stupefied as Maria picks up the pieces of the Virgin, carries the parts to the altar.

She turns slowly. Petra and Juliana take the pieces from her. Maria holds up her hand for silence. There is murmuring then a hush. Karl appears at the door of the chapel with his Reporter friend.

"In 1628 and in 1636 our order and the Virgin gave protection to this village against the outbreak of plague." Maria gets down on her knees in a prayer position. The rest of the Sisters likewise kneel. "This year, I ask the village to free us and the Virgin from this stupid charade. We ask you, God, end our suffering. No more prostrating and bowing to dumb idols in prayer and supplication! How many hours have we spent and how many gallons of tears have we wasted at the feet of idols." She looks up. "I bow my knees only to the Son of God, my Saviour, Jesus Christ. To Him be all glory, honor and praise, now and evermore. Amen."

The Sisters echo of "Amen" rings around the chapel.

*

Xavier Guttens is seated in a large chair in his opulent house. Maria stands before him attended by Harlindis and Juliana.

"I want the abbey lands back."

"You don't have anything to buy it back with."

"I have your son."

"What about my son?"

"There is a reporter from Antwerp waiting at the abbey to interview all of us. He wants to know about the abuses that have been going on in the convent.

"What's my son got to do with it?"

"Quite a lot. He has raped all three of us."

"Is this a joke?"

"We're not laughing. You have no idea what filthy habits your son learned when he was a priest." Guttens is lost for words. "How did you acquire the abbey lands? Through your son?"

"Yes, I did."

"While he has raping us?" Guttens is a decent man at heart. It is uncomfortable listening for him. "Shall we tell your wife before we tell the reporter?"

Guttens jumps up. "Enough! It shames me to hear this. I will transfer the lands back to the abbey! But I have conditions .... No mention of this meeting is to be made to anyone."

"Yes. What else?"

"My son is not to be reported to the police or his name appear in the newspapers."

Harlindis can't contain herself. "We can't accept that!"

"The priests you can drag over the coals for all I care. But my son ... he will answer to me. I am an honourable man, I will see you get your justice."

Maria assesses Guttens and his sincerity. "I give you one week to transfer the lands and show us your justice has been carried out."

"You have my word."

*

Xavier and Christien are armed with shotguns. Its is clear they are out hunting for small game. "You remember the first time you took me hunting, father?" Xavier is putting some shells into his shotgun. "We came into these woods. How old was I? Eight or nine?"

Christien puts his shotgun against a tree, takes out a cigarette, lights it. Xavier snaps shut the barrel of his shotgun.

"What am I going to do about Nina? I'm starting to get fond of the little brats. Nina's a nightmare, still. Do you think she'll ever grow up?" Xavier is walking towards Christien. Christien looks at his father advancing on him. "I hope that thing isn't loaded."

Xavier is within three metres of Christien. He levels the shotgun, pulls both triggers.

*

Choral music is heard. A car is in the distance coming towards to abbey.

The Sisters are gathered outside the main gate. Humbelina is watching the car coming towards the abbey.

The other Sisters are chatting excitedly. Idesbalda, Roberta and Alberica are kicking a football about. Humbelina shouts "Tell Maria he's here." Roberta runs inside. Alberica goes to follow her but Humbelina takes her by the hand, makes her stay to watch the approaching car. Alberica smiles.

Harlindis exits holding a small bag.

Maria exits behind her. She is dressed in a plain black suit skirt and jacket. Her hair is bobbed. In her hand is her caliper. She hands it to Harlindis in exchange for the small bag. Rosa, now in full nun's clothing thrusts a bible into Maria's free hand.

"Thank you, Rosa."

Harlindis is straining to see the car.

"Is your father really going to be in the car?"

"Yes, I believe he is."

Juliana exits with Heleen and is carrying a wrapped up parcel.

"What's this Juliana?"

"Heleen and I stole a few hours from prayer to knit some things for you.

Pink and blue. You never know."
Juliana places her hand on Maria's
stomach. Maria is visibly moved.
The car pulls up. The Sisters swarm
around it, try to see inside. Juliana
laughs. "They are like children."
"Make sure they get out more."
"I will." Juliana hugs Maria.
Maria makes towards the car
followed by Juliana and Rosa.
"Maria!"
Maria turns. Petra is now Mother
Superior. "You must promise to
visit?"
"And you must promise to visit me
in Rotterdam, Petra." They embrace.
"Be kind to the girls. The old ones
too. They have nowhere else to go."
Sister Agnes and Lucia are
sheepishly standing just within the
gates.
Maria turns and gets into the front
of the car. Her Father, an elderly
man, takes her little bag and parcel
and puts it on the back seat. He
pushes on the horn.
The sound makes the Sisters stand
back in fear. They fall into laughter
at their own silliness.
The car turns around. The Sisters
wave feverishly as the car pulls

away.

Maria pushes her arm out of the window, continues to wave as the car recedes down road.

The Sisters wave back, start to drift back inside the abbey.

*

Xavier Guttens meets Nina and her children at the door of his large house. They are all dressed in mourning clothes. He ushers them inside. A blackbird settles on a tree, begins to sing.

ROBBIE MOFFAT

The author was born and schooled in Glasgow. He took a degree in English language and Literature at Newcastle University. He began writing when he was seventeen and has had a career as a poet, novelist, playwright and screenwriter. He is best known for his feature film work in which he is also a director and producer.

His prose writing as been overshadowed by this. He wrote his first novel when he was twenty two and continued to write novels for the next twenty years.

The rediscovery of his prose work has led to a recent spate of publications that has created a resurgence of interest in his prose writing.

BY THE SAME AUTHOR
available in paperback from Palm Tree Publishing

Lost In The Landscape
The Lost Summer
Lost In The Desert
Christine and Her Teachest
Helmut Razor – Serial Killer
The Loving
The Loving Child
The Loving Few
The Loving Many
Love The One You're With
The Great Getaway
Glasgow Boy
Rage Against The Light

*

Printed in Great Britain
by Amazon

57278397R00058